Three  nd the C...ree

A Katherine Baker Adventure

By Jocelyn Porter

Illustrated by Clare Caddy

First published in the UK in 2016 by
Bromleigh House Ltd
The Old Lodge
48 East Street
Newton Abbot
TQ12 1AQ

Text copyright © Jocelyn Porter, 2016
Illustrations copyright © Clare Caddy, 2016
'Cupcake Kate' is a trademark of Bromleigh House Ltd.

Acknowledgment
Thanks to Helen Greathead: Editorial Adviser

A CIP Catalogue record for this book is available from the British Library.

ISBN: 978-1-909714-57-1

Printed and bound by CPI Group (UK) Ltd, Croydon, CR0 4YY

For Rosa Marie
A Daydream Believer
JP

For Scarlett, Reuben & Matilda
...who add the sprinkles to my life
CC

The Buttercup Bakery

Main Street, Puddington

My Bedroom

1832

BUTTERCUP BAKERY

BAKERY

CAFÉ

CAFÉ OPEN

This is where I live

Me and My Best Friends

We're in the same class at
Sunnymead School

Contents

1   A Perfect Nickname   9½   ...1   8·70

2   Coffee and Cakes   ...17   5·48

3   Cooking Is Magic!   ...29   6·50

4   A Window that Winked   ...41   6·28

5   The Naming Game   ...53   6·10

6   The Treasure Hunters   ...63   7·40

7   With a Huff and a Puff   ...77   7·34

8   Cuckoo, Cuckoo!   ...89   6·50

9   A Big Surprise   ...101   6·24

10   Little Cupcake Superstar   ...113   6·30

11   Moonglow Magic   ...125   5·22

12   Cupcake Mischief   ...135   9·50

28·16 m

28·12 m

28·06

151

+30

80   1 hr 25 m approx

3 × Approx 28 m + menu.

S: 456 = 7·5

m .77

8·4·5

A Perfect Nickname

"Dad, what *are* those men doing?" I squawked, pointing to two strangers who were wandering round the garden hammering wooden posts into the ground. "And why have they got that long tape measure?"

"You mean the builder and the architect?" Dad replied. "They're measuring the garden for our new kitchen."

1

"*What* new kitchen?" I yelped. "No one's told *me* about a new kitchen."

"No, I'm sorry, we haven't had time yet," said Mum. "Dad and I only made the decision yesterday. We were going to tell you, but everything happened so quickly."

I was fuming. I hate it when Mum and Dad know something and they haven't told me. You would think I was still a little kid – I'm sure they forget I'm eight and a half.

"Snickerdoodles Mum, that wasn't fair," I said stamping my foot. "I don't like being the last to know."

"No sweetie, I know you don't," said Mum trying to calm me down, "but it's quite simple really. The bakery is so busy these days we need a bigger kitchen and that's why we're going to build one in the garden."

"You're going to build a kitchen in the *garden*?" I cried in horror. "You can't do that, I love our garden the way it is. I don't want a kitchen out there."

"Don't worry," said Dad, "the new kitchen is just an extension to our old kitchen. The lawn and vegetable plot *and* your precious orchard will still be there. You'll hardly notice the difference."

"Well I hope you're right," I said glaring at Dad, "because if you mess up the garden I'll leave home and go and live with Grandma."

"Okay Katherine," said Mum with a wink. "I'd better pack your bags then."

Mum was joking – I think – but I wasn't going to take a chance.

"No you won't," I said screwing up my eyes and frowning at her. "I've decided to stay – someone has to look after the garden."

Our bakery is The Buttercup Bakery on Main Street in Puddington. It's a very old building near the centre of town.

There's a shop and cafe on the ground floor and we live upstairs in a jumble of rooms. My bedroom is three floors up in the attic.

Mum and Dad are Bryony and Bob Baker and they're a perfect baking team. Mum makes cakes with delicious fillings, she whips up fantastic frostings and her sugarpaste designs are amazing.

Dad's croissants and bread rolls are too scrumptious to describe. His crusty bread is a Buttercup Bakery speciality – people queue to buy it hot from the oven.

I'm allowed in the kitchen when Mum and Dad are not too busy and I make cupcakes. It's so much fun – specially the decorating bit. I love swirling the buttercream and sprinkling the sugar stars – I get buttercream everywhere!

One day, when Dad was watching me bake, he burst out laughing.

"You're a funny little chip off the old baking block," he teased wiping a blob of buttercream from my chin. "You get more buttercream on yourself than on top of the cakes

– I think you'll turn into a cupcake one day," he said. "I'm going to call you Cupcake Kate from now on – it's a perfect nickname for someone who enjoys making cupcakes as much as you do!"

"You're right Dad," I said with grin, "it's delicious fun." Then I ran my finger round the bowl – and licked it!

The weeks went by and I forgot all about the new kitchen, until one morning I heard the squeal of brakes outside the bakery. I opened the lounge window and saw a lorry reversing up to the garden gate.

"Oh no!" I cried in horror as I stared down at workmen off-loading a cement mixer and piles of bricks.

"Mum! Dad! Send them away," I pleaded.

But it was useless. The builders were in the garden and the work had begun.

"It will only take a month or so and then we'll have a lovely new kitchen," said Mum.

"Don't care, don't want a new kitchen," I sobbed burying my head in a cushion.

"Come on sweetie," said Mum. She put her arm round me. "Be a big girl and look on the bright side."

"Go away!" I yelled. "There *is* no bright side."

"Oh yes there is," said Mum softly, "you're only eight and you're already a good cook. Think of all the cakes you'll be able to make when we have the new kitchen."

"I'm *eight and a half*," I retorted, but I was listening to Mum. She could always get round me when she talked about cooking.

"You make some funny mistakes but everything you cook seems to

8

turn out right in the end," she said. "I think you've got a magic touch when it comes to cooking."

"Do you Mum? *Really*? *A magic touch*?" I said sitting up. "Well cooking is magic – isn't it?"

I was getting excited and once I'd started to gabble I couldn't stop.

"You put ingredients in a bowl, stir them together and put a sticky mixture in the oven. You set the timer and when it goes *ping* the mixture has changed into a cake. It's like pulling a rabbit out of a hat. Cooking is a magic trick." I declared, finally stopping to take a breath.

I was still thinking about pulling a rabbit out of a hat when Grandma Daisy walked in to the lounge.

"Did I hear you and your mum talking about a magic touch?" she asked rubbing her nose. "Oh dear – I'm going to sneeze. Talking about magic always makes me sneeze – *ah… ah… tishoo!*"

Grandma flopped down on a chair in an untidy heap.

"See what you've done with your silly chatter? I'm all in a fluster now," she said pulling her skirt straight.

"There must be a fairy nearby
– there's magic in the air and it's
making my nose tickle. Have *you* seen
a fairy, Katherine?" she asked.

"No I haven't," I said shaking my
head vigorously. "I don't believe in
fairies."

"That's a pity. I do," said
Grandma. "Only a fairy can give you
a magic touch – and *only* when you
deserve it. *Atishoo!*"

"That's nonsense," I snapped,
"and *do* stop sneezing Grandma."

"I'll leave you two to sort this
out," said Mum. "I haven't got time to
argue about fairies, there's too much
work to do."

When Mum left the room
Grandma gave me a long, hard look.

"Right Katherine, just listen to

me," she said. "I know you'll meet a fairy one day and when you do she will cast a spell on you. Then you will have your magic touch."

"That's silly talk Grandma," I groaned. "I'm too old for fairy stories. Just because you believe in fairies doesn't mean I have to."

"No, it doesn't, but if your favourite chef said he believed in fairies I'm sure you'd believe *him* wouldn't you? Toby Clark has a magic touch when he cooks on television doesn't he?"

"Yes he does. He's a wiz of a cook but not because a fairy cast a spell on him," I protested. "Look – I'll show you, his show is usually on catch up the morning," I said grabbing the remote control.

I switched on just in time – the
programme had started and Toby
Clark was about to introduce his
guest to the audience.

"I'd love to be a guest on his
show," I said. "Can you imagine what
a thrill it would be to cook with Toby
Clark on TV?"

"Not really," Grandma replied
with a chuckle, "but I'm sure you can.
I think you fancy being a television

star, you've always been a bit of a show-off, haven't you Katherine?"

"No I haven't," I snorted indignantly. I was quiet for a minute or two and then shrugged my shoulders.

"Well, perhaps I have, just a bit, but everyone wants to be on television these days, don't they? Charlotte wants to be an actress and Sophie wants to be a singer, so you see, it's not just me – it's my friends as well."

"That may be true," replied Grandma, in a tone of voice that implied she disapproved of such things, "but not everyone has the talent to be on television, do they Katherine?"

"Well Toby Clark certainly has.

If I ever meet him I'll ask him if he believes in fairies. I'm quite sure he won't — but then I'm also quite sure I'm never going to meet him — so it doesn't really matter," I said with a sigh.

Grandma chuckled. "You never know Katherine, you might — one day." Then she started to sneeze again.

5.48
5.54

5.52

Chapter 2.
Coffee and Cakes

I spend a lot of time with Grandma
when Mum and Dad are busy in the
bakery – and they are always busy
in the bakery. They never have much
time to talk to me these days.

As soon as the new kitchen was
ready Mum and Dad filled it with
mixers, ovens, freezers, fridges and
all sorts of things I don't even know
the name for. I have to admit it

17

looked pretty amazing – all shiny and bright. I couldn't wait to get in there and start baking.

As well as new equipment, new people arrived too. It turned out they were a waitress and a cook about to start work in our bakery. Mum and Dad found plenty of time to talk to them!

Not long after the kitchen opened I had a bit of a disaster – well it was quite a big disaster really. There was something I wanted to ask Mum and I could see her on the other side of the kitchen.

Mum didn't see me and I was too impatient to wait. I ran across the kitchen without looking where I was going and bumped into the new waitress.

Her tray went flying and cups of coffee and a plate of cakes crashed to the floor. Everyone stared at me. I felt terrible!

"You're lucky no one got hurt," scolded Dad as he chased me out of the kitchen.

Dad and I had a long chat about 'health and safety' rules after that. Dad said a busy kitchen is a dangerous place and he was banning me until I could act in a more grown-up way.

"I don't think the kitchen is a dangerous place," I muttered. "It's people who are dangerous – they get in my way."

Dad ignored that comment and when I complained that Mum was always too busy to talk to me he ignored that too. His mind seemed to be on other things!

I was cross with myself for being so careless and really sad about being banned from the kitchen. At least I'm still allowed in the shop and cafe.

The smell of coffee and delicious cake drifts from the cafe and floats down Main Street. It attracts customers to the bakery all day long. It's like an invisible string pulling them in.

The Buttercup Bakery is a favourite meeting place for the celebrities of Puddington. They sit and chat for hours over their coffee and share all the latest showbiz gossip.

Reporters and photographers pop in to the bakery from time to time just to see who's in town. When they spot a celebrity they don't hesitate for a second, they take a quick snap, make a few notes and the photo appears in *The Puddington Daily News* the very next day.

Celebrities like having their picture in the newspaper and The Buttercup Bakery is definitely the best place in Puddington to be seen.

The other day I heard excited voices coming from the cafe and I ran to see what was happening. Customers were huddled in a group and a photographer was trying to take a picture.

There was obviously someone interesting in the middle of the commotion but I couldn't see who it was because too many people were in the way.

"Who's going to be the guest cook on your next show Toby?" shouted someone in the crowd.

"Toby...? It must be Toby Clark," I squealed with excitement. *Grandma was right,* I thought. *She said I might meet him one day.*

"I don't know who'll be on the next show," I heard Toby protest. "It's always a last-minute decision. The guest cook could be anyone – that's what makes the show fun."

"I wish it could be me," I muttered, "but that's *never* going to happen. Who wants to watch a kid cooking on television?"

The noisy chatter went on and

on and with so many fans around
Toby Clark I didn't stand a chance of
talking to him. I was getting irritated.

"Toby, do you believe in…?" I
started to call from the back of the
crowd – but my hand shot up and
covered my mouth before I could
finish my sentence.

"D'oh – that was a silly thing
to say," I muttered and ran out of the
café and into the garden. What if Toby
had heard me? I was horrified at the
thought; it was a daft idea to ask him
about fairies.

I was angry and when I came to
a pile of leaves I jumped right in them
– even though Dad had brushed them
up.

"Flippity flapjack, life's not
fair," I moaned as I kicked the leaves.

"I finally have a chance to meet
Toby Clark and everyone gets in
my way. Got that wrong, didn't you
Grandma?" I shouted. "You didn't say
anything about silly customers getting
in my way."

I spent the rest of the day in
a deep, dark sulk but by the next

morning I'd calmed down and when I went down for breakfast there was a surprise waiting for me.

"Look at this Katherine," called Mum. "There's a picture of your favourite chef in *The Puddington Daily News*… and guess what – he was in our cafe."

"Yes, I know he was – I was there too," I moaned, "but I never got a chance to talk to him."

"Never mind sweetie," said Mum giving me a cuddle, "just think of the positive side – it's fantastic publicity for The Buttercup Bakery. If Toby Clark comes here for coffee his fans will want to come too. I expect we'll be busy today."

"Well, that's your problem," I replied in a rude, *I don't care,* sort of way. But then I gasped in surprise.

"Oh look Mum! It's me," I squealed pointing to the photograph in the paper. "You can just see me at the very back — behind all the customers. Ooh, do you think Toby will come in again? I do hope so. I won't let anyone get in my way next time."

COOKING
SPELLS

Marigold Moonglow

Chapter

Cooking Is Magic!

"Yikes, what was that?" I yelled as something whizzed past my head. "What *are* you doing Grandma?"

Sometimes Dad calls Grandma Dizzy Daisy. He says it with a giggle so I know he doesn't *really* mean it. What I don't understand is why Dad thinks I'm safer in Grandma's kitchen than the bakery kitchen. Just shows how much he knows!

I ducked again and you'll never guess what actually whooshed over my head – only a flying frying pan! It was zooming round Grandma's kitchen like an angry wasp.

"Do you like my new frying pan?" asked Grandma with a grin. "It can toss pancakes all by itself. Watch this."

The frying pan hovered, did a quick flip and a pancake flew into the air. It shot straight up and got stuck on the ceiling.

"Oh dear," said Grandma with a giggle. "I haven't quite got the hang of it yet."

"Grandma, you're crazy… you've finally flipped," I yelled, grabbing a plate as the pancake plopped from the ceiling. "Stop playing with that frying pan. Someone might get hurt," I scolded.

"Happy now, are we?" said Grandma as the frying pan landed on the cooker. "You're a real scaredy-cat, Katherine."

I put the plate on the table and prodded the pancake with my finger.

"It's soggy," I groaned. "What a useless frying pan! Where did you get it?"

"It was a present from my best friend," chuckled Grandma. "I think it's great!"

Grandma lives in Willow Cottage on Laburnum Lane and Laburnum Lane runs right behind Main Street – which is where we live.

It is very easy for me to visit Grandma. All I have to do is walk

to the bottom of our garden then
through the door in the garden wall
and I'm in the garden of Willow
Cottage.

Grandma has a Siamese cat
called Cocoa. He's very handsome
but there's something odd about
him. He parades along the garden

wall with his nose in the air and his sapphire blue eyes darting from side to side. Nothing escapes his attention. Cocoa's the king of the castle at Willow Cottage.

Grandma talks to him all the time and she says Cocoa talks to her but I've never heard him say a single word, although I've heard him meow a lot.

"It's the mayor's annual cake competition is in a few days," said Grandma. "I'm making cakes to sell on the fund-raising stall. Are you going to help me? They're collecting money for Sunnymead School this year."

"Yes, of course I'll help," I said, "but why does the school need money?"

"To repair the roof, it's a bit leaky," said Grandma.

"I'd rather go on a trip to the zoo or the seaside," I said. "That would be worth making cakes for."

"And so is a leaky roof," said Grandma. "You don't want to do your lessons under an umbrella, now do you?"

"Yes I *do* Grandma. That would be fun."

"I don't think your teacher would enjoy it," said Grandma. "Come on, let's get on with our work." Grandma pointed to a book on the kitchen table. "I'm sure we'll find a recipe you like in here, it's full of delicious ideas."

"Who's Marigold Moonglow?" I asked reading the name on the cover. "I've not heard of her before."

"She's my best friend and she's a *fabulous* cook," said Grandma proudly. "I went to Sunnymead School with Marigold."

"Did you?" I gasped. I'd never thought of Grandma as a schoolgirl before. I tried to imagine her in school uniform but couldn't, it was too ridiculous for words.

"Well, I go to Sunnymead School with Sophie and Charlotte. I've got *two* best friends," I said proudly.

"I know you have, and I hope you stay friends with both of them for ever. I've been friends with Marigold nearly all my life. Real friends are very special people."

"I know they are Grandma," I said, "but I want to know why *your* best friend called her book *Cooking Spells* and not just recipes? Does that mean she's a witch? I might have guessed you'd have a spooky friend."

"You're being silly now Katherine," scolded Grandma.

I ran my fingers over the title on the book. I hoped it might have spell-like abilities – perhaps it would twinkle or glow, but it did *nothing* … it was a fraud.

"Did Marigold give you that ridiculous flying frying pan?" I asked. "Only a spooky friend would give you a present as crazy as that."

"Marigold's not spooky," protested Grandma, "but yes, she

did give me the frying pan. It was a surprise present."

Grandma sighed and went all dreamy. "Marigold gave me Cocoa a few years ago, he was *such* an adorable little kitten," she cooed.

"Well he's not adorable now, he plays mean tricks on me," I complained. "Marigold is spooky and so is Cocoa."

"Well, spooky or not, Marigold came to see you the day you were born. She gave you a kiss on your cheek," said Grandma.

"Yuk!" I groaned pretending to rub the kiss away.

"It was a lovely sunny day. You do remember it, don't you?" asked Grandma.

"Of course I don't, I was only

one day old," I said throwing my arms in the air. Grandma can be quite exasperating at times.

Something was puzzling me though. Why did Grandma's best friend – someone I don't know at all – come to see me when I was one day old?

I knew I wouldn't get an answer to that question so I asked about the book again.

"Come on Grandma, tell me why Marigold called her book *Cooking Spells*?" I insisted.

"That's easy. Who said cooking was a magic trick?" chuckled Grandma poking me in the ribs. "It was you Katherine, wasn't it?"

"Might have been," I replied cautiously, wondering what Grandma was going to say next.

"Well, Marigold says the same thing. She says cooking is magic so recipes must be spells. It makes perfect sense to me."

I thought for a long time before I dared to ask the next question. It had been rattling round in my head for ages but I still had to force the words out of my mouth.

"Grandma, *you* do strange things sometimes," I croaked. "Are *you* a witch?"

"Cocoa, did you hear that?" exclaimed Grandma holding her head in her hands. "Katherine thinks I'm a witch – she thinks I do strange things. How *utterly* outrageous is that?"

"Meow-ow!" was Cocoa's reply.

The Window that Winked

Grandma stroked Cocoa and Cocoa licked her hand.

"Cocoa says I shouldn't listen to your silly nonsense Katherine," said Grandma with a grin, "so I'm going out. I need some fresh air. We'll talk about cakes for the mayor's fund-raising stall later."

Off went Grandma and I was left alone in the kitchen with Cocoa.

Grandma was up to something, there was no doubt about that, but I had no idea what.

I was wandering round the kitchen looking for something to do when a cupboard door flew open. I jumped and banged my knee on a chair.

"Ouch," I yelled. "That hurt."

I was rubbing my knee when I saw something out of the corner of my eye. A plate floated out of the cupboard and landed on the table.

"That didn't happen," I muttered to myself as a shiver ran down my spine. "It was just my imagination."

Seconds later I knew it was real because a box of cat food followed the plate out of the cupboard and hovered above the table.

Cocoa jumped on the table and flicked the tip of his tail. The box immediately tipped over and kibbles poured on to the plate.

"Purrrrow," purred Cocoa.
"Just wait till Grandma sees what you've done," I told him. "You'll be in trouble when she gets home!"

Cocoa ignored me and started to munch his food but I was determined to have the last word.

"Grandma *does* do strange things Cocoa," I insisted. "She talks to you and the trees and sometimes her hair stands on end, I've seen it. Grandma says it's caused by static electricity *and* she says it tickles. I think that's strange even if you don't."

Cocoa turned his head and growled at me.

"Don't you dare disagree with me you... you... uppity cat," I snapped. "It's bad enough having a Grandma who does strange things without you doing magic tricks. Who do you think you are," I huffed. "Cocoa the Magician?"

"Hello Katherine," boomed

Grandma as she bounced back into the kitchen. "Is everything all right?"

"No!" I complained. "You startled me charging in like that."

"I see Cocoa's been up to his old tricks," laughed Grandma as she moved the plate of cat food. "Anyway, I've come home for a rest. I've been rushing around all morning."

I looked at the kitchen clock. As far as I could see Grandma had only been away for about ten minutes.

"We'll look for cake recipes tomorrow. I want to sit in the garden for a while now."

With that Grandma wandered outside with Cocoa trotting behind her. I followed and plonked myself on the swing. I was in a mega strop! I didn't believe Grandma had been rushing anywhere. She was just making an excuse to sit in the sun.

Grandma sat on her garden lounger with a hat over her eyes.

"I'm going to have a cat-nap," she mumbled from under a big floppy brim. "Don't disturb me."

"I won't," I snapped back, "as long as that crazy cat of yours doesn't annoy me."

"Don't worry – he's wandered off for a cat-nap himself," muttered Grandma and she gave a loud yawn.

I love the swing in Grandma's garden – it hangs from a branch in the old oak tree and when I swing on it the air rushes through my hair and I feel as light as a feather. I think I could swing right up to the stars.

I'd only been swinging for about

five minutes when I began to feel uncomfortable. It was not a nice feeling at all.

"Grandma," I squealed. "I've got prickles all over my scalp. I'm sure someone's watching me."

"What did you say?" gasped Grandma knocking her hat on the floor as she suddenly snapped awake. "Who's watching you?"

"I don't know. I can just feel it," I complained.

"Well, look at your bedroom window and tell me what you see," said Grandma.

I could just see my bedroom window from Grandma's garden. It was three floors up in the bakery roof.

There are two windows in my

47

bedroom, one at the front and one at the back. I've given names to both of them.

The one I can see from Grandma's garden I call Dolly Daydream, because it has a big window seat where I sit and daydream.

I gaze at the garden below and imagine I'm flying with the birds as they swoop through the trees in the orchard. My imagination is better than any roller-coaster ride.

I call my other window Tommy Tiptoes because I have to stand on a box on the tip of my toes before I can see out. I don't look out of this window very often.

I was still staring at Dolly Daydream when she did something quite extraordinary. It took my breath away.

"Oooh Grandma, Dolly Daydream just winked at me!" I gulped.

"Really?" said Grandma with a knowing smile. "Well, if you insist on naming your windows maybe you have to live with the consequences. Your bedroom is obviously keeping an eye on you."

"Now you're being silly again," I said. "My bedroom can't keep an eye on me – it's not alive."

"No, it's not alive like you and me," agreed Grandma, "but it's alive in its own special way. The Buttercup Bakery is such an old building, lots of strange things happen there."

Grandma has a way of saying

49

things that makes me want to believe her. I don't always understand what she means but it usually sounds exciting.

"Wouldn't it be great if Ettie Spaghetti was alive?" I said. "She's the best rag doll in the world and I've had her for as long as I can remember. Do you know why I call her Ettie Spaghetti, Grandma?"

"Oh, that's a tough one. Let's see if I can work it out," said Grandma pursing her lips. After a long pause she said, "Could it be because her hair looks like spaghetti?"

"Bouncing blueberries, Grandma, I never thought you'd guess! But it doesn't matter – at least Ettie's hair is not like yours. Sometimes your hair stands on end.

50

Ettie's hair doesn't do that!" I said.

"It might," teased Grandma, "you never know what Ettie can do. I expect she's dancing round your bedroom with Teddy right now. Those two get up to all sorts of things when you're not there."

"That's nonsense!" I said, but curiosity got the better of me and I flew to the door in the garden wall. "I'll see you later," I shouted.

I ran through the orchard and across the lawn. I glared at the new kitchen as I passed by and bounded at full speed up three flights of stairs to my bedroom in the attic.

6.10

Chap 5   7mm
.3

The Naming Game

I stood outside my bedroom door and took a deep breath. I'd puffed myself out rushing up the stairs. When I stopped panting I slowly opened the door and peeped into my room.

Everything looked normal – except for a big bump in the middle of my bed.

I ran across the floor and grabbed my duvet.

"Gotcha," I cried as I dragged the duvet off my bed, but to my surprise I found Ettie Spaghetti hiding there.

"Ettie," I squealed as I picked her up. "I left you sitting on my chair. How on earth did you get under my duvet?"

I heard a meow and looked round. Cocoa was curled up on the window seat snuggled into Teddy.

"So that's where you sneaked off to Cocoa," I said. "Grandma said you had gone for a cat-nap."

Cocoa looked at me through half-open eyes, stretched his legs and managed to knock Teddy on to the floor.

"Oh Cocoa, you clumsy cat, Teddy wouldn't like that," I scolded.

Cocoa twitched his whiskers

and jumped off the window seat. He walked across the floor, flicking the tip of his tail as he went, and when he got to the door he turned round and stared at me.

He had a look on his face that seemed to say, *So Teddy fell on the floor... wasn't my fault... get over it.*

"Cocoa, you are *so* annoying," I shouted after him as he scooted down the stairs, but he ignored me – as usual.

I put Teddy back on the window seat and patted his head.

"Never mind Teddy," I said. "It's a good job you've got a nice round tummy to land on! Sit in the sun with Dolly Daydream for a while."

I went back to my chair and hugged Ettie. I whisper all my secrets in her ear – her rag-doll head must be full of my thoughts.

"I wish you could talk Ettie – you could tell me what's been going on in my room."

I love my topsy-turvy bedroom. I'm sure it's the cosiest bedroom in the whole wide world, especially in winter when there's a fire in the grate."

I sighed and looked around.

"There's not a straight line anywhere, Ettie," I murmured. "The walls are wobbly and the ceiling slopes down to the floor. If Grandma is right and my bedroom is alive – in its own special way – I suppose I'll get used to it."

Something was preying on my mind and at first I couldn't work out what it was – then it dawned on me.

"I know what it is Ettie," I said, jumping to my feet. "When Dolly Daydream winked at me, Grandma said it was because she had a name – so I'm going to name everything in my room. Perhaps they will do funny things too, ooh wouldn't that be fun?"

I walked to the fireplace and ran my fingers along the mantelpiece.

"What shall I call my fireplace, Ettie? Do you think Felicity is a good name?" I asked. "Felicity Fireplace sounds very grand… and Pinkie for my chair… what else could I call a pink armchair? And Dotty for my spotty rug will be good."

I skipped across to my bed. "You've got to be Bella," I said. "You make me feel like a princess. You're the softest bed there ever was."

Twirling round my room I felt as fizzy as popping candy – I was dizzy with happiness.

"Nearly done Ettie," I said. "You and Teddy already have a name and so do Dolly and Tommy but I'm sure I'll find more things to name tomorrow. My room seems extra special now – don't you think?"

A cool breeze blew on my arms and made me shiver. I saw my curtains flapping. Dolly Daydream was wide open. I put Ettie on the chair and ran to close the window.

"Dolly, did you open by yourself?" I said. "I don't remember doing it." I closed the window and made sure the latch was secure. "Is this your way of saying thank you for your new friends? Please don't open by yourself again Dolly," I scolded. "What if Teddy fell out?"

As I turned round Felicity Fireplace blew puffs of smoke into my room.

"Felicity, there's no fire in your grate today. What *are* you doing?" I protested.

Oh dear, I sound like Grandma. I'm talking to a window and a fireplace, I said to myself.

Grandma was right – strange things were happening in my bedroom. The new names must be working already.

"Stay on Pinkie Chair this time Ettie," I said as I hurried to the door. "I'm off to find Grandma."

I ran downstairs, across the garden and through the door in the garden wall.

"I think you are right about my bedroom, Grandma," I panted when I saw her still sitting on the sun lounger.

"You only *think* I'm right?" she said in surprise. "Don't you know for sure? When I saw your window open and puffs of smoke popping out of the chimney I thought something important had happened."

"I'm confused Grandma," I confessed. "I want my bedroom to be alive – in its own special way – I really do, but I don't understand how that happens."

"I don't think anyone knows *how* it happens – it just *happens*. Some places are special," said Grandma. "If something feels alive to you then it *is* alive. Trust your instincts and you can't go wrong."

"I hope you're right," I sighed, "because I've given names to my fireplace and my chair, my rug and my bed. It made me feel happy – I'm sure it was the right thing to do."

"That's good. You trusted your instincts," said Grandma.

"Yes, I did, didn't I?" I replied

feeling proud of myself.

Then I gasped. In all the excitement I'd nearly forgotten that Sophie and Charlotte were coming to play after lunch.

"I'm not going to tell them about my bedroom. I want to get used to it myself first," I said.

"I think that's a wise decision, so why don't you make something nice for your friends? Some cupcakes perhaps? It will keep you busy while you wait – and it will take your mind off your bedroom," said Grandma.

"That's a good idea. I'll make cherry cupcakes – they will be perfect," I said.

"Of course they will," said Grandma with a twinkle in her eye. "You'd better start right away."

The Treasure Hunters

I raided Grandma's cupboard and found everything I needed for my cupcakes. I beat the butter, sugar and eggs until they were fluffy. I sifted the flour and stirred the batter, then folded in the cherries with a dash of vanilla essence. Cooking makes me tingle with happiness.

It's the best thing ever, I thought to myself.

"These cakes smell delicious," I called to Grandma when I took them from the oven. "I'm going to cover them with buttercream, add a sprinkle of sugar pearls and a shiny red cherry on top. I love decorating cupcakes."

When they were finally ready, I stood back to admire my handiwork.

"Wow, they're so pretty," I said in delight, "just like blossom time in the orchard. What fun."

"Thank you Katherine," said Grandma, scooping the cupcakes into a cake box. "I'm off to see the mayor. Your cupcakes will go nicely with his afternoon tea."

"Bubble and squeak Grandma, that's a rotten trick," I squawked as my cupcakes walked out of the door with Grandma. "Those cupcakes were for my friends, not the mayor."

I felt as flat as a pancake after Grandma had gone and mooched around feeling sorry for myself. But as soon as Sophie and Charlotte arrived everything changed. I cheered up right away.

The three of us are in the same class at Sunnymead School, so in term time I see them every day, but it was the school holidays and I'd not seen them all week.

"Let's go to my den," I said. "The orchard will smell wonderful on a sunny day like this. I know it will be a good day for treasure hunting."

My den is an old wooden shed deep in the trees. It smells like warm apple pie and honeysuckle and is as snug and cosy as a den should be.

We have beanbags to sit on and a table for a picnic… it's a perfect hideaway for my friends and me.

We'd just flopped down on the beanbags for a chat when there was a tap on the door and Grandma peeped in.

"Hello girls," she called. "I've brought you some freshly baked doughnuts from the bakery."

Grandma put a plate on the table and that was an invitation we couldn't resist.

"Thanks Grandma," I said as we dived in. "Is this your way of saying sorry for pinching my cupcakes? I hope it was worth it. Did the mayor enjoy them?"

"Yes he did," replied Grandma. "He said they were *amazingly* good. He was surprised someone your age could make such *very* good cupcakes."

"Was he?" I said. "Well that's nice. I'll make him some more one day – if you ask me, instead of just pinching them."

"Sorry about that Katherine, but

they looked so nice. It was a spur of the moment thing – if I'd asked you to bake cupcakes for the mayor they may not have turned out so well," said Grandma. "But I'm sure he'd like some more when you feel like making them."

"We're going treasure hunting in the orchard right now," I said. "We're looking for buttons and beads and all sorts of shiny things. You'd be surprised what we find in the roots of the trees."

"Nothing you find would surprise me," said Grandma. "This orchard was here long before The Buttercup Bakery was built and The Buttercup Bakery was built a very long time ago."

"Was the orchard here when the

dinosaurs were around?" piped up Charlotte. "We've not found any old bones yet."

Grandma raised her eyebrows. "Not quite *that* long ago Charlotte," she said with a laugh, "but woodland people used to live in this orchard and I'm sure they must have left one or two things behind."

Grandma had an impish grin on her face and then she started to sneeze.

"Oh dear. Must have pollen up my nose," she said. "See you later Katherine, enjoy your treasure hunt."

Grandma wandered off sneezing her way through the trees.

"I wonder who the woodland people are," I said. "I've never heard Grandma talk about them before."

"Perhaps they're woodland fairies," said Sophie. "Woodland fairies are special you know. They're as big as people."

"I don't believe in fairies," I said with a humph.

"What do you mean? You must believe in fairies," said Sophie sounding shocked, "there are fairies *everywhere*."

"Like that witch creeping up behind Charlotte," I whispered.

"Don't be ridiculous," giggled Charlotte as she twirled round, "there's no witch behind me."

"Precisely," I said, "and there are no fairies either."

"You'll regret saying that," snapped Sophie. "Don't blame me if a fairy twists your tongue one day."

70

"You're pixilated," I said. "Let's forget about fairies and go treasure hunting."

We found three strong sticks and started searching through the undergrowth. We raked through the fallen leaves, poked our sticks under every root and peeped down every rabbit hole, but the only things we found were acorn cups and sycamore propellers.

We sent the propellers flying into the air and tried to catch them in the acorn cups. We finished up with a mound of acorn cups and sycamore propellers in our hair.

We'd been jumping around so much we were hot and tired when we came to the corkscrew tree. The grass below it was cool and dappled and we flung ourselves on the ground for a rest.

I always smile when I see the corkscrew tree. Its curious twisted branches curl higgledy-piggledy in a tangled knot. It looks as if it has just got up and forgotten to brush its hair.

Buttercups and mushrooms grow in the green moss between its roots like the sprinkles I scatter on my cupcakes.

I rolled over and looked up through the branches and to my surprise Cocoa was looking back at me.

He was playing with a leaf dangling from a twig. Cocoa whacked the twig with his paw and it fell to the ground, followed by Cocoa who jumped out of the tree and scurried away with a leap and a bound.

While I was watching Cocoa, Sophie and Charlotte had been watching the twig and saw it land in a clump of mushrooms.

"Oooh look!" squealed Sophie. "There's something shiny under those mushrooms – right where the twig landed. Can you see it Katherine?"

"I think so," I said wriggling forward on my tummy. "I'll hook it out with my stick."

I gently maneuvered the shiny thing onto the end of my stick and flicked it out. It sailed through the air twinkling all the way, and landed at Sophie's feet.

"Treasure," squealed Sophie as she picked it up. "We've found treasure!"

"It's gold," gasped Charlotte as the thing shone in Sophie's hand.

"Let's go back to my den and look at it properly," I said jumping up and leading the way.

Back in my den we stood and stared at our shiny gold treasure. We were in shock. We could hardly believe what we saw.

"It's a gold locket," I said in awe. "This is the best treasure we've ever found."

"*I* think it belongs to a woodland fairy," said Sophie jumping up and down with excitement. "What do you think?"

"I think a fairy lost it when she walked past the corkscrew tree," said Charlotte.

"I don't know what to think,"

I said, "but if it does belong to a woodland fairy she'll be very sad. I'd be sad if I lost something as beautiful as this."

I surprised myself – was I beginning to believe in fairies? No of course not, but the locket seemed to fascinate all of us.

A plan popped into my head.

"If we put my table outside my den and leave the locket on top a fairy might see it tonight," I said.

"That's a brilliant idea," said Sophie dancing with glee. "If the locket has gone in the morning we will know a fairy found it."

Chap 7

With a Huff and a Puff

The next morning I ran down to the orchard to see if the locket had gone.

"Oh, galloping goosegogs," I squeaked, "it's still there!"

I wasn't sure whether I was pleased or sorry. I was getting used to the idea of fairies, but as I carried the table back into my den I decided I was pleased no one had claimed the locket.

If it had gone we would never really know if a fairy had taken it. Magpies pick up shiny things you know.

"I'll tell Sophie and Charlotte later," I thought. "No doubt they'll come up with some new theory about who owns it."

As I walked back to the bakery the lawn looked soft and inviting, in a warm, sunny, daydreamy way, so I decided to stay a while.

I lay down on the grass and closed my eyes. I imagined I was in a magical world where dreams come true. I was making cupcakes on *The Toby Clark Show*. The studio lights were on and the cameras were rolling.

When Toby Clark walked into my daydream everything was perfect, but moments later the lights went out and my perfect daydream was shattered.

"Hey! Who did that?" I yelled.

I jumped up in a fury only to discover it was the sun that had been switched off – well it had disappeared behind the only cloud in the sky.

"You nasty cloud," I shouted. "You've ruined my daydream."

The sun appeared again and I watched as the cloud floated slowly down until it was hovering above my head. I hadn't expected that at all.

I felt uneasy. I prefer clouds that stay in the sky. I would have run away but my legs refused to move, so I had to stand there and stare at it.

"What do you want, you horrible cloud?" I cried.

The cloud twirled round and that's when I caught sight of a face. It was not very clear but it was definitely there, hiding in the cloud.

"With a huff and a puff I'll blow sugar sprinkles all over you," said a mischievous voice from the cloud.

The cloud took a deep breath

and then gave a huff and a puff and sugar sprinkles rained down on me. I was covered in them from head to toe.

"Why did you do that? I'm not a cake," I complained brushing the sprinkles from my clothes.

"Yes you are," said the voice in the cloud gurgling with laughter. "A little bird told me your father calls you Cupcake Kate. He says you will turn into a cupcake one day because you get more cream on yourself than on the cupcakes. You're a teeny-weeny daydream girl, a Cupcake Kate in a creamy whirl."

The cloud seemed very pleased with itself and jiggled around.

"I like that," declared the voice. "Teeny-weeny daydream girl ...

blah, blah. It's a good tongue twister Katherine. See how fast you can say it."

"No I won't," I snapped. "I don't like tongue twisters and I don't like you. I'm *not* going to say it."

"Spoilsport," said the voice, "but if you won't play tongue twisters with me I'll twist your tongue instead."

The cloud huffed and puffed again and blew bubbles all over me.

I had to giggle because the bubbles tickled my nose and went into my mouth.

"They taste like lemon drops," I

said out loud.

"Yes they do. Have fun with your twisted tongue Katherine," called the voice from the cloud before it shot away into the sky.

"Just wait till I see Sophie," I shouted. "If I've got a twisted tongue I'll blame her. She started this twisted tongue business."

I'd never met a talking cloud before and I was confused – it didn't seem normal at all. I was glad when I heard Grandma calling me.

"Katherine, come here, I've something to tell you," she called and I didn't need asking twice, I sprinted as fast as I could to Willow Cottage.

I plonked myself on a chair, glad to be in Grandma's kitchen, but I didn't say anything – just in case my tongue really was twisted.

Cocoa wasn't helping the situation either – he was in a silly mood. He was doing his best to annoy me.

"Cocoa, stop showing off," said Grandma.

"Don't want to," said Cocoa jumping on my knee flicking his tail across my nose. "It's fun annoying Katherine and I've nothing better to do at the moment!"

I was totally shocked! I heard every word that Cocoa said.

"Cocoa nac klat," I said excitedly, tugging Grandma's sleeve.

Grandma just stood there and laughed.

"You're talking nonsense Katherine, your tongue's in a twist.

What were you trying to say?"

"Cocoa *can* talk, I heard him," I said.

I was relieved the words came out the right way this time but my tongue *was* twisted – and that was terrible!

"I'm pleased you can hear him. It was bound to happen sooner or later," said Grandma.

"What was bound to happen?" I asked in an irritated voice.

"You being able to hear Cocoa," replied Grandma. "Everything can talk if you keep your ears open and listen."

"That's ridiculous," I said.

"I can see sugar sprinkles in your hair," said Grandma. "Where did they come from?"

85

"From a cloud," I groaned. "It floated down to the garden and rained sugar sprinkles all over me."

"Well, that explains it," laughed Grandma. "You've been caught up in a sprinkle spell. Now you can hear the world around you. There are voices everywhere you know!"

"I don't believe you Grandma," I said. "That's just another of your silly tales."

"Oh, you'll soon get used to it." Grandma said. "Talking to the things around you is the most enormous fun."

"Well I suppose it could be," I said grudgingly. "But what did that cloud do to me?"

"The cloud did nothing. It must have been Marigold – cloud flying," replied Grandma.

"Cloud whating?" I exclaimed

"Cloud flying. It's one of Marigold's funny old tricks," said Grandma. "She jumps in a cloud and flies round the sky. She must have seen you in the garden and decided to cast a sprinkle spell on you."

"Is Marigold a fairy then?" I asked. "You said a fairy would cast a spell on me and give me a magic touch one day. Have I got a magic touch now?"

"No you haven't," said Grandma emphatically. "You will know when that happens. By the way, that twisted tongue of yours, did Marigold cast a bubble spell on you as well?"

"Well the cloud rained bubbles on me, if that's what you mean," I said. "They tasted like lemon drops."

"That accounts for it then – the bubble spell is one of Marigold's most annoying tricks. Your tongue might trip you up again when you least expect it."

"So she's not a fairy, she's a mean old tongue-twisting witch," I moaned.

"Marigold's not mean Katherine, you must stop jumping to conclusions," Grandma insisted.

"Trampolines and jelly beans, I'll jump to as many conclusions as I want," I wailed.

6.5°

Chap 8

Cuckoo, Cuckoo!

"Go on then Katherine, jump," said Grandma. "I'll sit here and watch you. You'll soon get tired."

I was fuming but Grandma was grinning and I began to feel silly.

Grandma had said talking to things would be fun so I decided to calm down and try it.

"Can Ettie talk like Cocoa?" I asked.

"Yes, of course she can," replied Grandma, "and so can Teddy... and who knows how many more."

"Marshmallow munchies," I whooped. "Miserable Marigold can't spoil that."

I was about to run off when I remembered Grandma had something to tell me.

"What was it you wanted to tell me, Magrand?" I asked. "Is it portimant? Oh dear, there I go again, I mean – is it important Grandma?"

"Yes it is, but after all this excitement I'll wait until tomorrow to tell you."

"No, tell me now please, you're gnitsaw emit – whoops – I mean, you're wasting time."

"No Katherine, tomorrow will

be fine."

"Dumpling stew," I moaned, "I'll be wondering what you want to say all day."

"No you won't," said Grandma. "Go and talk to Ettie Spaghetti. That will keep your mind on other things. Just be up bright and early tomorrow and I'll tell you what I have to say."

I ran to my bedroom with my heart beating like a drum.

"Ettie, talk to me, please," I called as I rushed into my bedroom. "I know you can."

I picked up Ettie and hugged her tight.

"Ouch," squealed Ettie. "You'll squeeze all the stuffing out of me."

"Sorry," I gasped in horror. "I didn't mean to hurt you."

"Don't worry, you didn't. I'm used to being hugged," said Ettie.

"Ettie Spaghetti I love you so much," I said.

"I know," said Ettie, "and I love you too."

"Don't forget me," called Teddy from his perch on the window seat.

"Of course I won't," I said. I put Ettie on my bed and rushed over to give him a kiss.

"Hello Katherine," said Dolly Daydream.

"Hello Katherine," echoed Tommy Tiptoes and Felicity Fireplace from the end of the room.

"Welcome to our magical world," called Bella and Pinkie together and Spotty Dotty, my rug, just laughed.

"Hello everyone," I called. "I'm so happy. Marigold cast a sprinkle spell on me and now I can hear you all." I yelled punching the air.

Something was pulling my skirt, so I looked down. Ettie was standing there all by herself.

"My goodness, you can walk as well as talk," I gasped.

"Sometimes we dance all day and sometimes Cocoa comes to play," said Ettie. "Now you've been *sprinkled* we can dance and play with you too."

"Yes we can," said Teddy running to join us, "but only in this special room and only when you're on your own. When your friends come to play we won't be able to do a thing – the magic only works when you're alone."

It had been a most amazing day and my bedroom would never be the same again.

When it was time to snuggle down in bed I felt as if I was floating on a cloud.

"Sleep tight Katherine," whispered Bella. "Thank you for my lovely name."

Oh happy me!

The next morning I was up bright and early and raced down the garden and into Grandma's kitchen. I was bursting with curiosity. I wanted to know what she had to tell me.

"I've got a surprise for you," said Grandma. "Guess what the mayor had to say?"

"Well, you've already told me he liked my cakes," I said. "What else did he say?"

"He thought your cupcakes were so delicious he wants you to enter the cake competition," beamed Grandma.

"Does he?" I said. "Crispy crackers! I'm only eight – well eight and a half actually – I thought I was too young to enter."

"Of course you're not too young," said Grandma. "Choose a cake spell from Marigold's book – there's bound to be one you like."

Grandma placed the book on the kitchen table and it opened by itself. It seemed to be in a very chipper mood today.

"Hello Katherine," said the book flipping over its pages one by one.

"Hello," I replied nervously. I wasn't expecting the book to talk, but then why not, so many other things do!

"Time to get started," said the book. "Marigold's cooking spells are tiffin terrific."

"What would you like to make?" asked Grandma. "One big cake or a plate of cupcakes?"

"Well, as my nickname is Cupcake Kate," I replied, "it has to be the cupcakes."

"How about this one?" said
the book stopping at a spell called
'Butterfly Cupcakes'.

"Mmm," I said as I read the
ingredients. "I love it… orange and
lemon zest and cream cheese frosting
with sugarpaste butterflies for
decoration. It's perfect!"

Grandma had already made her
cakes for the fund-raising stall and
she started to decorate them while I
collected my ingredients.

I made my batter and all was
going well until it was time to add the
vanilla essence. I grabbed the bottle
and sploshed a drop into the cupcake
mixture.

"Bubbling bourbons, I've picked
up the wrong bottle," I cried in

dismay. "I've put rose water in my batter instead of vanilla essence. I've ruined it! There's no rose water in this spell. I'll have to start all over again."

"Do you have enough time?" asked the book.

I glanced at the clock on the kitchen wall and the cuckoo flew out and shook his head.

"Cuckoo, cuckoo," chirped the bird.

"Botheration," I said. "I know I'm a silly cuckoo, you don't have to tell me. Whatever shall I do now?"

"No problem," said the book. "Just read the spell again."

And there it was as plain as it could be – vanilla *and* rose water.

"You've added your own touch

to the butterfly cupcakes," said the book, "so I've added rose water to the spell. The butterflies will like that, they love roses."

"Thank you," I said. "You are a clever old book."

While my cupcakes were in the oven I made the sugarpaste butterflies and gave them rose-red spots on their pretty white wings.

"They're beautiful," I said. "They look so real."

"Well done Katherine," said Grandma as she admired my cupcakes. "Now it's time we were on our way to the town hall."

A Big Surprise

I felt proud and really grown-up as
Grandma and I carried our cakes to
the town hall.

Grandma's cakes went onto the
fund-raising stall for people to buy,
but my cupcakes were put on one of
the competitors' tables. There were
lots of cakes on lots of tables and they
all looked wonderful.

It must have been a very special

It must have been
very special

day because Mum and Dad took an
hour off work to come and see me
and I got a lovely squidgey cuddle
from both of them.

"Are you sure my cupcakes
are good enough to be in the
competition?" I asked Mum. "The
others look much better than mine."

"Well, *I* don't think so," said
Mum. "I think your cupcakes look
perfect."

"And so do I," said Dad. "You're
a very clever girl."

There were all sorts of cakes
in the competition – fruit cakes,
birthday cakes, wedding cakes... I
wandered round the town hall by
myself looking at them in amazement.
I was in cake heaven.

"Ladies and Gentlemen," called

the mayor as he appeared on the stage. "Please give a big Puddington welcome to celebrity chef Toby Clark. Toby is the judge of our cake competition this year."

There were cheers all round as Toby Clark stepped forward and waved. I was so excited I could hardly catch my breath. I scurried back to Mum and Dad who were waiting for me at the cupcake table.

"Toby Clark is going to judge my cupcakes," I twittered. "Oh dear whatever shall I do? I never expected that."

"You don't have to do anything," said Grandma. "Toby's already judged the cupcakes. He did it while you were looking at all the other cakes."

"Oh bother, I missed him again," I moaned

I moaned.

"Don't fret," said Grandma. "Competitiors are not allowed to watch their entries being judged anyway."

I heard voices calling me and twirled round so quickly I nearly fell over. To my surprise I saw Charlotte and Sophie waving like mad.

"We thought we might find you here," called Charlotte.

"Where there's cake you'll always find Katherine," said Sophie with a laugh.

"Well I'm glad you're here – you'll never guess what I've done," I said.

Charlotte and Sophie wriggled through the crowd and we hugged and giggled.

"Look!" I said pointing to
my cupcakes. "I've entered the
competition and I'm so nervous –
Toby Clark has judged my cakes."

"Oooh – you clever thing," said
Charlotte.

"They look scrumptious," said
Sophie. "Can I have one?"

"Later – when the competition
is over. I said

is over," I said.

The mayor and Toby Clark walked back onto the stage. Toby had made his decisions.

"The winner of the fruit cake category is…" started the mayor.

"… Mrs Eccles!" finished Toby Clark. He presented Mrs Eccles with a bottle of champagne and a big bouquet of flowers.

"Mrs Eccles always wins," whispered Grandma. "She adds ginger and figs to her sticky fruit cake."

Mrs Plum was next to be called to the stage. Her birthday cake was a winner. It was covered in sugarpaste flowers and colourful dots, with a big bow and lots of candles on the top.

Toby Clark gave Mrs Plum her bouquet and bottle of champagne and everyone clapped.

After a few more presentations Toby Clark and the mayor slipped away from the stage and went to talk to Mum and Dad. It was all very odd, but Toby and the mayor were back on the stage before I could get too curious.

"Ladies and Gentlemen," said the mayor, "we now move on to the cupcake category."

I reached out for Sophie and Charlotte. I was shaking like mad.

"It's my pleasure to announce the name of the winner… our youngest competitor, Miss Katherine

Baker," said Toby Clark. "Her butterfly cupcakes are as light and delicate as butterflies themselves. They're quite magical."

I gasped out loud and Sophie and Charlotte squeezed me tight. I never dreamt I would actually win.

"Katherine Baker entered the competition for the first time this year," said the mayor. "She's not just our youngest competitor, she's our youngest ever winner."

Everyone cheered and I could feel myself blushing. It got even worse when Toby Clark called me up onto the stage.

"Congratulations. Well done Katherine," said Toby Clark, "or should I call you Cupcake Kate? Your father tells me that's your nickname."

Oh dear, I went all dithery. Toby
picked up a bouquet of flowers and
waved it in the general direction of
the audience.

"I'm sure you don't want this
bouquet Katherine," he said, "so I'm
going to give it to your Grandma
– she deserves it for encouraging you
to enter the competition."

Grandma looked quite flustered as Toby jumped off the stage and handed over the flowers with a kiss on her cheek.

"Now Katherine," said Toby as he leapt back onto the stage, "we have another problem. I can't give you the bottle of champagne because you're *far* too young so I'll give that to your mum and dad for having such a talented daughter."

Toby reached forward and passed the bottle to Dad. Oh dear, that popped my bubble. I felt quite deflated. I'd done all the work and my family got the prizes.

I was about to yell rhubarb mizzle – because that's what I say when I'm really cross. Luckily, before I could make a fool of myself, Toby

Clark started to speak.

"I've got a surprise for you Katherine," he said. "It's a very special prize and I hope you will like it."

"I'd like any prize right now," I muttered under my breath.

"I've had a word with your mum and dad and we've agreed that *you* will be the guest cook on my next television show. What do you think?"

"Me? A guest cook? On your show?" I gabbled. "I'd love that. I've always wanted to cook on your show but I thought I was too young."

I was shaking, my knees were knocking and I could see Mum and Dad clapping like mad.

"Thank you – that's the best prize in the world," I stuttered.

It took a long time to dawn on

It took a long time to dawn on me

me what had happened. My prize was a very *big* surprise indeed – the best prize I could have ever wished for.

"Good! That's all sorted then," said Toby. "I'll see you next week at the television studios. You'll be the star of my show."

Little Cupcake Superstar

I was still in shock when I got home
from the cake competition. The
thought of being on *The Toby Clark
Show* had sent me into a whirl.

"I'm going to be the guest cook
on *The Cloby Tark Show*, I'm such a
bappy hunny Grandma," I said dancing
around the kitchen. "I can hardly
believe it!"

"Your tongue's in a twist again,"

said Grandma. "I told you that might happen. We'll have to sort it out before you go on television. We can't have our prize-winning cook talking gibberish, can we?"

"I'm not galking tibberish," I said and then I gasped. "Oh dear, I am, aren't I?"

"Yes you are," said Grandma, "but I know how to get rid of your twisted tongue. Marigold used to twist my tongue when we were children – she could be very annoying sometimes."

"Well, she's not changed much, has she? She's still annoying," I said. "Why did she twist your tongue? What did you do to her?"

"Me? I don't think I did anything," said Grandma looking

114

innocent. "I might have put a few worms in her lunchbox but I didn't deserve a twisted tongue for that, did I?"

"You were as bad as Marigold, Grandma. You were both very naughty," I said with a grin.

At last I could imagine Grandma in school uniform. What a scary thought that was! I shook my head to get rid of the image.

"Hurry up Grandma, tell me how to cure my twisted tongue. I don't want to mess up when I'm on the telly."

"I've not done it for years but I'm sure it will still work," said Grandma. "You have to skip three

115

You have to skip 3

times around the corkscrew tree and say *Tizzy wizzy corkscrew tree untwist my twisted tongue for me."*

"Yako, Drangma, it sounds fike lun," I said. "I'll try anything to get rid of my twisted tongue."

I ran to the orchard and went straight to the corkscrew tree. Its crazy twisted branches seemed more twisted than ever. I skipped three times round the tree chanting the untwisting rhyme.

"*Tizzy wizzy corkscrew tree untwist my twisted tongue for me,*" I sang out loud. Then I skipped round the tree again because it was so much fun.

"Hello Katherine," called Dad as he walked into view. "Whatever are you doing?"

"Hello Dad," I replied. "I was just skipping for joy because I'm so excited about *The Toby Clark Show*!"

I know that was a little white lie but I couldn't tell Dad the truth, could I? I just hoped I really had untwisted my tongue.

"My cakes will look wonderful on the television," I said. "I'm going to make you and mum so proud," I said as Dad and I walked back to the garden.

"I'm sure you will," said Mum as she joined us on the lawn, "but we're already proud of you."

"Grandma encouraged me to enter the cake competition," I said. "Do you think she's proud of me too?"

"I'm sure she is," said Dad.

I suddenly remembered the little gold locket and realised I hadn't told Grandma about it yet.

"Well, I'm off to see Grandma now," I said and ran to Willow Cottage with a hop, skip and a jump.

"Grandma, when we were treasure hunting the other day we

found a gold locket," I said. "It was under a mushroom in the roots of the corkscrew tree. Sophie thinks a fairy might have lost it."

I told Grandma what we'd done and that the locket was still on the table the next morning.

"I know who that locket belongs to," said Grandma. "She'll be so pleased you found it."

"She? Who does it belongs to Grandma?"

"It belongs to Marigold. She lost it the other day when she came to visit me."

"Bah! Cheese sticks and garlic dips – I wouldn't have got so excited if I'd known it was Marigold's."

"Well, no matter what you think, Marigold will be very happy

You found it

you found it. Would you get it and bring it to me? I will keep it safe for Marigold," said Grandma.

I was about to wander back to the orchard to get the locket when I remembered I had something important to say.

"Thanks for encouraging me to enter the cake competition Grandma," I said plonking a kiss on her cheek. "I'd never have won without you."

"I'm very proud of you," said Grandma. "You made some excellent cupcakes – and Marigold will be proud of you too. She likes to keep an eye on you."

"I don't know why she does that. I wish she would go away. I don't want her to spoil my day."

"She won't, I promise you, now go and get her locket and we will all be happy," said Grandma.

So many exciting things happened the next week that once I'd given the locket to Grandma I completely forgot about it.

I went to the television studio to see what I had to do. The floor manager showed me Toby's kitchen. I was surprised to find it was just two walls with no ceiling. There were lots of lights dangling from beams above the stage and when they were on, the kitchen looked so real.

Cookers and fridges were set in the walls and a shiny work surface faced the audience.

There were just six rows of seats – not many at all – but they were

There were just 6 rows of seats - not many at all - but they were close to the kitchen, so everyone would be able to see what I was doing.

The floor manager walked me through my moves with the cameraman and the lighting technician. I felt like a real star.

There was a window at the back of the set that looked out over a garden — or so I thought. When I ran over to look through it I discovered it wasn't real at all.

There was no glass in the window frame, the plants were in pots and the trees were painted on screens.

That's television! I said to myself, smiling. *Nothing is quite what it seems to be.*

I thought Toby Clark was never

going to turn up but right at the end of the day he breezed in to the studio.

"Hi there my little Cupcake Superstar," he called. "All ready for the big day are we?"

"Yes," I said. "I'm so excited. I'm really looking forward to it."

"Good! That's what I like to hear," he said. "I'm looking forward to it as well. You'll be a big hit with the audience I'm sure."

Me? A big hit? I could hardly believe my ears. Toby Clark actually said I'd be a big hit! And he called me his *Little Cupcake Superstar* – nothing gets better than that.

Toby signalled to the floor manager and they sat down to discuss the show. Tomorrow couldn't come soon enough.

Moonglow Magic

I rushed home to tell Grandma all about my day at the television studio, but when I arrived at Willow Cottage she was already talking to someone in the kitchen.

"Come in, Katherine. I want you to meet my best friend," said Grandma in an excited voice. "This is Marigold Moonglow," she proudly declared. "She has come to see you."

"Hello Katherine," said
Marigold. "I'm pleased to see you face
to face. You can't get a good look at
someone when you're inside a cloud
you know."

"Well, I'm not pleased to see
you. You were mean to me. You
twisted my tongue, you nasty old
witch," I snapped.

"Oh dear, do you really think I'm a witch?" gasped Marigold in horror.

"Of *course* I do!" I shouted.

"Katherine! Don't be so rude," exclaimed Grandma. "Say sorry to Marigold at once."

"Shan't," I snorted.

"Poor Katherine, I didn't mean to scare you," said Marigold gently, "but you were such a pompous little poppet when we met in the garden I couldn't resist teasing you. I'm definitely not a witch though, I'm a woodland fairy."

I have to admit Marigold didn't look like a witch. She looked lovely — even if her clothes were a bit *unusual* — but how was I to know if she was telling the truth?

"Some woodland fairies choose to live in the human world but I've always known Marigold was a fairy," said Grandma. "She threw sugar sprinkles over me when we were children, that's when I discovered her secret."

"You should have told me Marigold was a fairy, Grandma," I complained.

"Not just any fairy," said Marigold. "A very special fairy – I'm your fairy godmother."

"Wow! I didn't know I had a fairy godmother. That's another thing Grandma forgot to tell me!" I moaned.

"She didn't forget Katherine, she told you the day you were born – that was the day I gave you a magic kiss.

You *do* remember, don't you?" said Marigold with a twinkle in her eye.

"Not really," I sighed.

"Well, here's something you will remember," said Marigold. "I'm going to cast a spell on you. Are you ready?"

I nodded nervously and Marigold began to chant,

"Flibberty gibberty magicus,
Get ready for your magic touch,
Scrumptious goodies you will make
Every time you start to bake."

"Is that all?" I asked — rather disappointed. "I didn't feel a thing."

"No, that was just the warm-up chant, it's the next bit that's important," said Marigold grinning from ear to ear.

Marigold took a handful of sugar pearls from her pocket and threw them in the air. The pearls hovered in a shimmering cloud just above my head. They looked quite magical as they floated there.

"There's a moonbeam inside every pearl," said Marigold.

A voice in my head was saying, *Nonsense, they're far too small to hold a moonbeam,* but I didn't say a word. I just gulped instead.

"Snippety clickety," Marigold said, and snapped her fingers.

A moonbeam shot out of each sugar pearl and I was covered from head to toe in a twinkling glow.

"I'm tingling all over," I squealed running my hands through the moonbeams. "It feels like soft silver rain, all fizzy and bubbly."

"Tickles, doesn't it?" laughed Grandma. "That's Moonglow magic and static electricity rolled into one. Now you have your magic touch Katherine."

"There really *was* a moonbeam in each sugar pearl," I said in awe and hugged Marigold.

"Yes there *really* was," agreed Marigold, "and now we're going to celebrate with pancakes. There's nothing quite like pancakes with sugar and

lemon to Tickle your tastebuds

lemon to tickle your taste buds."

Marigold clapped her hands and Grandma's flying frying pan whizzed into the air.

"I've got the hang of this now," Grandma said. "Pancakes are on the way!"

"Marigold is a bad influence on you, Grandma," I giggled.

"Thank you for finding my locket," said Marigold pulling the locket from her pocket. "I lost it the other day when I was talking to the corkscrew tree – I've been friends with that tree since I was three."

"Have you," I said, although I wasn't surprised. "Grandma talks to the trees. Did she learn that from you?"

"I hope so," said Marigold.

"Everyone should talk to the trees – happy thoughts travel round the world on the breeze."

"Can I tell my friends about you, Marigold?" I asked. "They will be excited when I tell them the locket belongs to my fairy godmother."

"Yes, of course you can," said Marigold. "Sophie and Charlotte sound like great fun – you are lucky to have such good friends. I'm sure I can arrange something delicious and magical for you all to do."

"Thank you Marigold, that would be fantastic!"

The next day I was going to the television studio to record *The Toby Clark Show* so I had to concentrate on that. Telling my friends about Marigold would have to wait.

Cupcake Mischief

"Quiet everyone," called the floor manager as the audience settled in their seats. "We're ready for the first take."

I could see Grandma and Marigold sitting in the front row and Ettie Spaghetti was peeping out of grandma's bag.

"Hello Ettie," I whispered under my breath. "What a lovely surprise to

135

see you here."

Ettie's grin looked wider than ever and her eyes seemed to twinkle in the studio lights. I knew she could hear everything that was going on.

"I thought you'd be pleased to see Ettie Spaghetti," whispered Grandma lifting Ettie onto her knee."

I smiled nervously when the studio lights went up and my tummy started to churn.

Keep calm, I said to myself, *the butterflies are supposed to be on your cupcakes, not in your tummy. Anyway, what can go wrong? Now I've got my magic touch my cupcakes are bound to be perfect.*

Toby Clark walked onto the set and was greeted with a loud cheer. He introduced me to the audience and the audience cheered me too.

Toby Clark is a real superstar. I watched in amazement as he prepared his dishes. He called me over to help whip the egg whites for his meringue.

Toby made everything look so easy. Did you know he can cook and talk to the camera at the same time? He even joked with the audience while he put cream and strawberries on his meringue.

After a while it was my turn to cook and the cameraman focused on every move I made. I put the ingredients in my mixing bowl and stirred until the batter was silky smooth.

Toby came over and talked to me while the camera zoomed in on my face. That was scary but Toby kept smiling and winking at me when no

ond was lookugou, to I must love been dong Semething riant !!

137

one was looking, so I must have been
doing something right.

While my cupcakes were in
the oven I made the cream cheese
frosting and started on the sugarpaste
butterflies. The cameraman seemed
quite spellbound as he watched me
decorate the butterfly wings.

Even though I was nervous, my
cupcakes came out perfectly and as
soon as they were cool I began to

add the decoration. As I swirled the frosting on the cupcakes I felt that funny nervous flutter in my tummy again.

I could see Grandma and Marigold grinning and whispering to each other. I just knew they were up to something and my tummy fluttered even more.

I leant forward and frowned at them in a puzzled sort of way, but they didn't take any notice, so I carried on decorating my cupcakes.

As I placed the butterflies gently on top of the frosting I breathed a sigh of relief. My part in the show was nearly over.

I arranged my cupcakes on a cupcake stand and relaxed – big mistake!

Grandma and Marigold were smiling at me and Marigold was waggling her little finger in a funny sort of way. That's when things started to happen!

First one butterfly flapped its wings and then another and soon all the butterflies were flapping like mad. The cameraman gasped in surprise and tried to focus his lens on the cake stand but just as he zoomed in on the cakes the butterflies flew away.

"Hey Toby, look at this," he yelled but the butterflies

were so quick they flew out of the studio in a flash.

When Toby turned round there was nothing to see. Even the audience had missed the flying butterflies.

"Look at what?" called Toby.

"Sorry Toby, my mistake — it was nothing," spluttered the confused cameraman rubbing his eyes.

Grandma and Marigold were giggling like naughty schoolgirls — there was no doubt Marigold had put a spell on the butterflies and Grandma had encouraged her. I was furious with both of them.

"You may be able to make a frying pan fly round the kitchen Marigold, but you had no right to make my butterflies fly away," I hissed. "Now I'll have to make them

all agan ||

all again."

"We're off now Katherine," said Grandma. "You will be here for ages yet. They will need more pictures of you with your cupcakes – and your butterflies – when you've made them again!"

I watched as Grandma tucked Ettie into her bag. What a story my rag doll would have to tell when she got home!

Marigold blew me a kiss and slipped quietly out of the studio with Grandma.

I smiled to myself. It was no good – I couldn't stay cross any longer. Grandma and Marigold may be impossible, but they *are* great fun.

I felt light-hearted as I made my second set of sugarpaste butterflies. With my new butterflies sitting proudly on the cupcakes my cake stand looked beautiful again. The show had gone well.

The cameraman came over and filmed my cupcakes.

"Katherine," he whispered as he took the last shot, "did I see your butterflies flutter around the studio or did I imagine it?"

I wasn't sure what to say so I blurted out the first thing that came into my head.

"It must have been your imagination. Sugarpaste butterflies can't fly," I whispered back.

"Oh," said the cameraman and

he looked so disappointed that I felt sorry for him.

"Well, perhaps they did fly," I said softly trying to cheer him up. "There might have been a fairy in the audience who cast a spell on them."

"Do you really think so? No, that's silly," said the cameraman, "I don't believe in fairies."

"Neither did I until I met one," I said.

"That must have been exciting," said Toby as he came up behind us and joined in the conversation.

"Yes it was exciting," I agreed timidly.

"I met a fairy once," said Toby winking at me. "It was a long time ago but I saw her again tonight. She was sitting in the front row of the audience, chatting to a friend."

"Bah – stuff and nonsense," said the cameraman. "I didn't see a fairy in the front row."

"That was Marigold Moonglow," I squealed and burst out laughing. "She's my fairy godmother."

"And she's the best cook I know," said Toby. "Her cooking spells are tiffin terrific."

"That's what the book said," I gasped as I remembered the day I made my competition cupcakes.

"I've got a copy of Marigold's *Cooking Spells*," said Toby. "I wouldn't be without it."

Well, who'd have thought it, Toby Clark does believe in fairies after all. What a perfect end to my perfect day.

The show was over and as soon as I arrived home I sent a text message to Sophie and Charlotte. *Come round — got a secret to share.*

Sophie and Charlotte arrived in a flurry, they were in such a hurry to find out all about the show. We chatted for a while about Toby Clark and the studio kitchen and everything I could remember. Although I'd loved every moment of the show I was bursting to tell my friends about Marigold.

"Do you remember the gold locket we found in the orchard? Well, I've found out who it belongs to."

I paused…

"Come on," said Charlotte,

"Who? Who?"

"You sound like an owl, Charlotte," laughed Sophie, "but tell us Katherine, please."

"It belongs to a fairy," I whispered.

"Told you so. Told you so," squealed Sophie jumping up and down.

"Yes you did," I said, "but you didn't know the fairy was *my* fairy godmother, did you?"

Sophie stopped jumping and Charlotte just stared at me. For once they were both lost for words.

"My fairy godmother is beautiful and funny and she's called Marigold Moonglow. She lost the locket when she was talking to the corkscrew tree," I said.

147

"Marigold wants to meet you. She's promised to arrange something delicious and magical for us to do. Would you like that?"

"Yes! Yes! We *really* would," screamed Charlotte and Sophie and we laughed and jumped round my bedroom until we could laugh and jump no more.

I woke up the next morning buzzing with happiness and ran downstairs tingling from head to toe.

"Well, well," said Dad peering at me over his newspaper. "What do you make of this Katherine? There's a picture of you on the front page of *The Puddington Daily News.*"

Dad gave a big smile. "Quite the little star – aren't you?"

"Yes she is, but not so little," said

Mum. "Katherine looks quite grown up in that photo."

I stared at the picture in disbelief. I never imagined I'd be in the paper. Not *just* me on the front page all by myself.

"I loved cooking on *The Toby Clark Show*," I said. "Being on television is fun. I'm going to have my own television show one day, when I'm older. Then I'll be a real star. I'll call my show *The Katherine Baker Show*. That will be exciting,

won't it

won't it?"

"Yes, it will, but you've got a lot to learn before you can be a celebrity chef like Toby Clark. Being a star doesn't come easy," said Mum.

"No, it doesn't," Dad agreed, "but you've proved you can act in a grown-up way and I'm proud of you."

"So am I," said Mum. "And Dad and I have something important to say."

Mum and Dad grinned at each other and came over and gave me a hug.

"We would like you to come and cook in the bakery kitchen again," said Dad.

"Would you like that?" asked Mum.

"Oh *yes*, I would," I squealed in

delight. "I'd like it very much."

"Dad and I would like it too. The kitchen has been quiet without your cheeky chatter," laughed Mum.

"Thanks Mum. Thanks Dad," I said as a great big grin spread across my face. "Being a television star is great fun but it will have to wait for a year or two. For now I just want to make cakes in the kitchen with you."